WILD HIKE

BY JAKE MADDOX

illustrated by Sean Tiffany

text by Chris Kreie

Librarian Reviewer
Marci Peschke
Librarian, Dallas Independent School District
MA Education Reading Specialist, Stephen F. Austin State University
Learning Resources Endorsement, Texas Women's University

Reading Consultant
Mary Evenson
Middle School Teacher, Edina Public Schools, MN
MA in Education, University of Minnesota

Impact Books are published by Stone Arch Books,
A Capstone Imprint
151 Good Counsel Drive, P.O. Box 669
Mankato, Minnesota 56002
www.capstonepub.com

Library of Congress Cataloging-in-Publication Data
Maddox, Jake.
    Wild hike / by Jake Maddox; illustrated by Sean Tiffany.
    p. cm. — (Impact Books. A Jake Maddox Sports Story)
    ISBN 978-1-4342-0785-2 (library binding)
    ISBN 978-1-4342-0881-1 (pbk.)
    [1. Hiking—Fiction. 2. Camping—Fiction.] I. Tiffany, Sean, ill.
II. Title.
PZ7.M25643Wi 2009
[Fic]—dc22   2008004300

Summary: Nick's cousins think he plays by the rules too much on their
camping trip. When they're in trouble, how will Nick react?

Art Director: Heather Kindseth
Graphic Designer: Kay Fraser

Printed in the United States of America in Stevens Point, Wisconsin.
092010
005957R

TABLE OF CONTENTS

CHAPTER 1

THE ROCKY TRAIL ★

"Hey bear!" shouted Nick. He clapped loudly as he walked along the hiking trail. The rocky trail was lined on both sides by tall green trees. "Hey bear!" Nick yelled again.

"Do you really have to do that?" asked his cousin Devin. Nick stopped and looked back. His cousins Andy and Devin were behind him on the trail. They both had large packs strapped to their backs.

"I don't have to. But it's a good idea to make a lot of noise while we're hiking," Nick said. "I'm doing it so we don't surprise any grizzly bears. Did you know that when people have trouble with grizzlies, it's usually because they sneak up on the bears by accident?"

Nick smiled. He loved talking about the outdoors. "The bears only attack when they're scared," Nick said. "If they know we're here, they'll stay away."

"Are you for real?" said Devin. "I thought this was supposed to be a vacation. You sound just like one of my teachers." Devin looked at Andy and laughed.

The smile disappeared from Nick's face. He put his head down and started walking again. He led his cousins farther down the trail.

The grass was still covered with dew. There was a chill in the morning air. Nick knew that even though it was July, the temperature was only in the forties.

As he walked, Nick looked around him. He looked at the blue skies, at the colorful wildflowers, and at a stream that flowed down a nearby cliff. Giant mountains stood in the distance.

"What is that jingling sound?" asked Andy.

Nick stopped. "Those are my bear bells," he explained. He held up his foot. The bells were silver and round, about as large as a quarter. "They're tied to my shoe laces."

"You've got to be kidding me," said Devin. "You look like one of Santa's reindeer." He laughed again.

"Grizzlies are all over around here," Nick said. "The bells help scare them away."

"That doesn't explain that can attached to your belt," Andy said.

"That's my bear spray," said Nick. "It's super powerful pepper spray, in case a bear actually attacks us."

"Let me get this straight," Devin said. "You're worried about a giant grizzly bear attacking us. And if it does, you're going to fight it off with some pepper spray?"

Andy laughed.

"It's nothing to laugh about," said Nick. "You're not in the city anymore. Out here, the grizzly is king. A grizzly bear can weigh 500 pounds. They have long, razor-sharp claws, and if they get angry, they will attack. You need to know this stuff."

"We want to see a grizzly!" said Andy.

"Yeah! Then we can impress everybody back home with our tales of strength," said Devin, showing his muscles.

"Get too close to one and you might not make it home," said Nick. "But if you want to come face-to-face with a grizzly . . ." He felt his face turning red with anger. Then he said, "I'm not going to stop you."

This trip wasn't Nick's idea. His dad and Uncle Teddy had come up with it. They thought a camping trip into Glacier National Park would be a perfect way for the three cousins to become closer.

Nick loved to camp. But camping with his cousins was another story. He didn't know Andy and Devin very well. Nick lived in Oregon. Andy and Devin lived in Ohio.

All Nick knew about his cousins was that they were huge and they were the best football players in their school. Plus, they were brothers and best friends.

"You'll get to know them," Nick's dad had told him. "That's the whole point. Their dad and I did a trip just like this when we were in junior high. You guys are that age now. It's about time you started doing more together. This camping trip will be great for the three of you."

Nick was starting to think his dad could not have been more wrong. Andy and Devin didn't seem to care at all about nature or camping.

CHAPTER 2

★ REFUELING

After they'd been on the trail for more than three hours, the boys climbed to the top of a flat rock. They looked out at a row of a dozen snow-covered peaks.

Directly below them was a field of grass and wildflowers. Beyond that was a thicket of skinny trees.

"Isn't it beautiful, guys?" asked Nick.

"Yeah, it's nice," said Andy.

"It's all right," said Devin. "But it's not as nice as Ohio Stadium, right, Andy? Sitting in the stands, watching the Buckeyes play football on a sunny fall day. Nothing beats that view."

"You got that right," said Andy.

Nick stared out at the mountains. He wanted to keep the picture in his head.

"Okay, let's go," said Nick. He started down the trail.

"Andy!" yelled Devin.

Nick spun around, expecting to see his cousin in trouble. But Devin just said, "Let's eat."

He and Andy reached into their backpacks. They removed water bottles, drink mixes, and candy bars.

"Again?" asked Nick. "This is like the fourth time we've stopped to eat. We need to keep going."

"We need to load up on food," said Devin. "We need to eat a lot so we can put on muscle."

"Yeah," said Andy. "And this hike is pretty tiring. We need to keep putting fuel in the tank, or we're going to go home skinny."

As the guys mixed their drinks and quickly swallowed their candy bars, Nick took a moment to look around. Then he noticed some movement in the thicket of trees several yards away. He looked closer.

A huge elk was walking slowly through the trees.

CHAPTER 3
★ SIMMER DOWN

"Hey, guys, come look at this!" Nick whispered.

Andy and Devin walked over to Nick. Nick pointed at the huge elk.

"Isn't she amazing?" Nick whispered. "It's very rare to see an elk in its natural habitat."

The boys watched as the elk nibbled green aspen leaves.

"Elks usually travel in herds," Nick told his cousins. "It's pretty rare to see one away from the rest of her pack."

"Thanks, Mr. Science," said Devin. "I thought we were on vacation, not in biology class!"

Nick tried to ignore him. "I'm surprised her calf isn't with her," he said. "Usually, the mother doesn't go far without it."

"How much do you think she weighs?" asked Andy.

"She's a big one," said Nick. "Could be 600 pounds or more."

The boys watched quietly. Slowly, the elk moved through the thicket.

"I'm going in for a closer look," said Devin. He picked up his pack and took out his digital camera.

"You're kidding, right?" said Nick.

"The zoom on my camera stinks," said Devin. "The elk would look like a little speck if I took a picture of it from here."

"You shouldn't get any closer," Nick told him. "She looks gentle and calm, but I bet she'll be pretty aggressive if she sees any of us. Especially if her calf is nearby."

"I don't see her calf," said Devin. He took another step toward the elk.

"Seriously, Devin," said Nick. "Getting closer is a really bad idea."

"Andy," said Nick. "Can you try to get through to your brother?"

"She looks harmless enough to me," Andy said, shrugging his shoulders. "I mean, who really cares if he gets in a little bit closer?"

Devin walked off the path and headed down toward the thicket.

"Devin," said Nick. "Stop. If she feels scared, she'll use her hooves to protect herself. Elks can do some serious damage."

"Simmer down," said Devin. "I think I can handle it."

Devin crawled toward the thicket. For a big guy, his movements were surprisingly smooth and quiet. The elk still had no idea that any of them were there.

Then Nick heard a noise. A skinny brown animal with long legs was coming down the path. It was the elk's calf. Nick nudged Andy in the ribs. Andy saw the calf and stepped back.

"Devin!" Nick called. He tried to shout and whisper at the same time. He didn't want to scare either elk.

But Devin didn't hear Nick. He also didn't see the calf walk up to its mother. Devin continued to crawl through the grass and flowers until he was just steps away from the mother elk.

Devin stood up and pointed his camera. Nick could hear the camera's click. "Gotcha!" yelled Devin.

The mother elk let out a loud shrieking sound. Then it raced away, through the trees. The calf panicked too, and charged after its mother. It ran past Devin, and missed hitting him by only a few inches.

"Wow, what a rush!" said Devin as he ran back toward the trail.

"That was awesome!" shouted Andy. "You're so lucky. You got so close!"

"Stupid, not lucky," said Nick.

"Nick, look at the picture," said Devin. "It's a real beauty." He held the camera in front of Nick's face.

"Yeah, it's great," said Nick. He shook his head. Then he lifted his pack onto his shoulders and started walking down the trail.

CHAPTER 4

MAKING CAMP ★

A few hours later, Andy and Devin dumped their packs next to a wooden bench and collapsed onto the ground of their campsite. Nick was right behind them. The three guys had made it to camp just in time. The sun would set soon.

"Finally, we're here," said Nick. "I'll get some supper going." Nick thought it was pretty funny to see his tough cousins so worn out at the end of the day-long hike.

After he sat down long enough to drink half a bottle of water, Nick pulled his cooking gear out of his pack. He removed a small cook stove from its bag.

Nick lit a match and held it to the stove's burner. The gas burst into a small flame.

Finally, Nick dumped a bottle of water into a metal pan. He placed the pan over the burner to boil the water.

"How come you can't just start a campfire?" Andy asked.

"There's a fire ban," Nick told him. "No open fires anywhere. It's too dry."

"Oh," Andy said. "Man, I'm exhausted."

"Not me," said Devin, lying on his back. "Get a little hot food in me and I'll be fine."

Nick smiled. The water boiled quickly. He opened three bags of freeze-dried meals.

"What are those?" said Andy.

"They're camping meals," said Nick. "All you have to do is add water and presto, instant dinner."

Nick poured some hot water into each of the bags. "They're actually pretty good," he told Andy. "I think you'll like them."

Finally, the food was ready. "Dinner is served," Nick said. He held out a bag for each of his cousins.

Andy and Devin each took a bag. Then Nick sat down and started eating.

"This smells nasty," said Devin. "What is this stuff?"

"It's turkey lasagna," said Nick.

"It smells gross," Devin said. He nervously took a bite. Then he made a face and said, "Yuck."

"Just eat it," said Andy, sitting down next to Nick.

The sun was setting by the time they finished eating. Nick knew they should start setting up the tents. "Let's make camp," he said, standing up.

"I don't feel like working right now," Devin said. "Let's go check out that lake we saw on the way here."

"Sounds good," Andy said. "It's only a five-minute walk away. Nick, do you want to come?"

"No, I want to set up my tent," Nick said. His cousins took off, running loudly through the woods.

About ten minutes later, Nick was almost done setting up his tent. As he pounded his last tent stake into the ground, Devin walked up behind him.

"It's getting pretty dark," Nick said. "You and Andy should get your tent up soon."

"We're not putting a tent up," said Devin. "We're going to sleep under the stars. Next to the lake."

Nick frowned. "I don't think that's a good idea," he said. "It's against the rules to sleep outside the campsite. It's dangerous. And I think it might rain tonight."

"They have rules for everything," Devin said. "And who cares about some clouds? The sky above us couldn't be clearer. Plus, the lake is really close to our campsite. If anything happened, we'd just come back."

Nick threw up his arms. "All right. I'm just trying to look out for you guys," he said. He finished hammering his tent stake.

"Do you know where I can get some firewood?" asked Devin.

Nick looked up. "Why?" he asked. "You know there's a burning ban."

"We just want to sleep next to a fire," said Devin. "We're not going to burn down the forest or something." He laughed.

Nick sighed. "You can't have a fire," he said.

"Why not?" asked Devin.

"Because of the fire ban," said Nick. "Anyway, even if there wasn't a ban, you would still have to keep your fire in the campsite fire pit."

"Whatever," said Devin. He turned and started walking back to the lake. "They really know how to spoil your fun around here," he called back. "This trip is no fun."

Nick sighed. He wanted to have fun too. But it was dark, so he had to finish setting up camp.

After he put up his tent, he started getting his gear ready for the night. He packed all the food and cooking supplies in a large nylon bag. Then he tied the bag to a rope. He threw the rope over a tree's branch and pulled the bag up into the tree. That would make sure no animals could reach it.

Nick had never set up a campsite alone before. He had always been with his dad. It was usually a fun part of the night, and when they worked together, it went quickly.

Once they were done, he and his dad always had lots of time for talking and watching for shooting stars.

Nick wished he wasn't with his annoying cousins. He felt left out, since he didn't know them well and he didn't play football. He also felt like he had to keep an eye on Andy and Devin or they'd burn down the whole forest.

As he stepped into his tent, Nick sniffed the air. Smoke was coming from a fire near the lake. He could hear his cousins' low voices and the crackling of the fire.

Devin was right. This trip was no fun. No fun at all.

CHAPTER 5

★ FINED

In the middle of the night, a clap of thunder jolted Nick from his sleep. Then raindrops started pounding on his tent's roof.

Seconds later, he heard Devin and Andy running up to his tent.

"Let us in!" Devin yelled.

Nick unzipped the door. Andy and Devin burst into the tent. They were both soaked.

They threw their wet sleeping bags on the floor of Nick's tent. Devin reached outside the door and pulled his backpack into the tent.

"Hold on," Nick said. "That has food in it, right?"

"Yeah, all our candy bars and stuff," said Devin.

Nick crawled to the door and threw the pack as far away from the tent as possible.

"What did you do that for?" asked Devin.

"Having food in the tent is like telling a bear to come in," said Nick. "We might as well just invite one in for a snack!"

Devin looked out into the darkness. "Great. Now I'll starve," he said. He shook his head and climbed into his sleeping bag.

After zipping the tent door closed, Nick squeezed back down onto the floor of his tent. Andy was on one side of him and Devin was on the other. The three guys were squished together like canned sardines inside the small two-man tent.

Within minutes, Andy and Devin were snoring. Nick sighed. *I hope morning comes soon*, he thought.

But it didn't. The night seemed to crawl by slower than any night Nick could remember. He passed the time by staring at the ceiling and listening to his cousins. Their snores seemed to grow louder by the hour.

At the first sign of daylight, Nick crawled out of the tent. Even though his watch said it was only 5:30 a.m., he was ready to start the day.

Nick pulled the nylon bag down from the tree limb and inspected the contents inside. Thanks to the plastic that lined the bag, everything had stayed dry during the storm.

He fired up his cook stove and boiled a pan of water. He added some of the water to a package of instant oatmeal. He poured the rest into a plastic cup and stirred hot chocolate powder into it.

As the sun rose, Nick ate his oatmeal and sipped his hot chocolate. The bad mood he'd been in the day before started to slip away.

Just then, he spotted a man coming down the trail toward their campsite. Nick peered through the trees. The man was wearing a park ranger uniform. And he didn't look happy.

Devin's fire, Nick thought. *The ranger must have spotted it.*

He knew his cousins' fire had been illegal, but he didn't want them to get into trouble. Nick stood up as the ranger walked into the campsite.

"Good morning!" Nick said, plastering a smile on his face.

"Good morning," the ranger said. "Can I see your camping permit, son?"

"Sure," Nick said. "It's right here." He looked in the nylon food bag and found the permit.

The ranger looked at the piece of paper. "I'm going to have to fine you for the fire your group had by the lake last night," the ranger said. He pulled a notepad out of his pocket and began to write.

"I'm sorry, sir," Nick said.

The ranger ripped the ticket out of his notepad and handed it to Nick. "This is a big deal, young man," the ranger said. "Next time, read the park rules and follow them. You could have caused a lot of damage with that fire. In fact, if it hadn't rained, you probably would have."

"Yes, sir," said Nick.

"All right," said the ranger. "You can pay that at any ranger station. Stay safe and be smart."

"We will," said Nick. The ranger turned and headed down the trail.

Nick looked at the ticket. He saw the number written on it and closed his eyes. "Two hundred dollars!" he whispered.

This trip can't get any worse, Nick thought.

CHAPTER 6

TIME AWAY ★

"What was that about?" Andy asked from behind Nick.

Nick turned. "We got fined," he said.

"Fined? For what?" asked Andy.

"For that fire you guys had last night!" said Nick. He walked back to the bench and sat down. He picked up the cup of hot chocolate. It was getting cold, so he added some more hot water.

"Sorry, man," said Andy. "How much?"

"Two hundred bucks," Nick told him.

"Devin and I will pay it," Andy said. "It was our fault."

Nick felt annoyed. It was nice of Andy to admit that it was their fault, but Nick just wanted to pretend nothing had happened.

"There's oatmeal if you want some," he told Andy.

Nick and Andy sat in silence for several minutes, eating their oatmeal. They watched as the sun climbed over a distant mountain peak.

"How do you know so much about camping?" asked Andy. "I mean, you know all about animals, how to cook, and all those rules and stuff. How do you know about all that?"

Nick took a deep breath. He was still mad. He stood up. "I know you didn't want to come on this trip," he told Andy. "You don't have to pretend to want to be here."

Nick turned around so he wouldn't have to look at Andy. He stuffed a granola bar and a bottle of water into his backpack.

"I'm going for a hike," he told Andy. "Don't start any more fires."

Before Andy could reply, Nick took off. He walked and walked, trying to get as far away from the campsite as he could.

It turned out the hike was just what Nick needed. He needed to be by himself, alone with the world around him and away from his cousins for a while. As he followed the flight of a hawk in the blue sky, he thought about what his dad had said.

"Your cousins may not be exactly like you," Dad had told him. "They may not love camping. But that doesn't mean you can't get along with them and have fun."

Nick hiked for over an hour. Finally, he reached the top of a large mountain.

It seemed like he was on top of the planet. Nick looked ahead at the trail in front of him.

A family of four mountain goats stood about a hundred feet away. They were nibbling on some grass just off the trail.

Nick decided to sit down and take a break. He wanted to be completely calmed down before heading back to camp. He was determined to give Devin and Andy one more chance, but he knew he had to be calm to do that.

For a while, he watched as the mountain goats moved slowly through the patch of grass. He wished his life could be as simple as the goats' lives were.

He waited a few more minutes. Then he let out a deep breath, stood up, and began walking back toward camp.

After another hour of walking, Nick rounded a bend in the trail and stopped. He was at the top of a hill, just a few minutes away from camp. Looking down into the valley, he could see the lake and the campsite below.

There was something moving in the field of tall grass next to the lake. Actually, there were two things. Nick squinted, but he couldn't quite see what the things were. He reached for his binoculars.

With the binoculars pressed to his eyes, he could see Devin. He was crouched over, walking slowly through the grass. Nick thought that the other moving thing must have been Andy. They were probably practicing football moves.

Then he saw that Devin was holding out a small object in his hand. *Oh no*, thought Nick. *What is he doing?*

Nick turned and scanned the field. The other creature wasn't Andy at all. It was a full-grown adult grizzly bear and it was standing just fifty yards away from Devin.

He's trying to feed it! Nick thought.

He couldn't believe what he was seeing. Nick panicked. He jammed his binoculars into his backpack and began to run toward camp.

CHAPTER 7
★ THE ATTACK

As Nick ran, all of his anger and frustration came rushing back.

He flew down the trail. He knew that he had to hurry. His cousins were in real danger, and they didn't seem to know or care.

It took five minutes for him to reach his cousins. Andy was at the edge of the meadow. He had the camera, and he was snapping pictures of Devin and the bear.

"What are you guys doing?" Nick said to Andy. "You're going to get killed!"

Andy just stared at him. He seemed surprised to see Nick. He didn't seem that worried that his brother was too close to a 500-pound grizzly bear.

Nick walked slowly and quietly into the meadow. He didn't want to surprise the bear.

The huge grizzly was still forty or fifty yards away from Devin. But that distance was nothing at all if the bear decided to charge.

So far, the grizzly looked calm. It seemed to be eating something growing in the field. It was totally ignoring Devin.

Nick walked silently toward his cousin. Devin noticed him and turned around.

"What do you think you're doing?" said Devin. "You're going to scare it away."

"Good," whispered Nick. "You need to get out of here."

"No, you do," said Devin. "You're going to wreck it."

"Wreck what?" asked Nick. "What are you planning to do?"

"I'm going to feed it," said Devin.

"Are you nuts?" Nick asked.

"Leave me alone," said Devin. Holding out a candy bar, he began walking toward the bear.

"Devin," said Nick. "Stop." But he knew it was just a matter of time before the bear noticed Devin. All Nick could do was stand and watch.

Devin kept walking across the meadow. Nick's heart was pounding.

Suddenly the bear turned its head. It looked at Devin and moved backward. That should have been a signal to Devin to stop. But he didn't stop. He kept moving forward.

The grizzly was staring directly at Devin, who was less than 30 yards from it.

"Devin," Nick said. "Get out of there." But Devin couldn't hear him. Nick was afraid to yell too loudly.

Devin held his chocolate bar low to the ground and began to slow down his movements. The bear began to look more and more nervous.

Suddenly the grizzly dropped its head low to the ground and made a loud noise. It sounded like a dog barking.

Devin froze in his tracks.

Nick had read books about grizzlies. He knew what they did when they felt threatened. A threatened bear would make eye contact, drop its head, and make a barking noise. These were classic signs that the bear was angry.

Nick feared what was coming next. Even though making noise might get the bear even more upset, Nick knew he had to warn Devin.

"It might make a bluff charge at you! That means it might run toward you but then it will stop!" yelled Nick. "It will just try to scare you. If it does make a bluff charge, just crouch down and look away from it."

The bear was barking louder.

"No way!" yelled Devin. "If he runs at me, I'm running away."

"No," said Nick. "That's the worst thing you could do."

The bear swung its head from side to side and grunted even louder. Then Devin did exactly what he wasn't supposed to do. He turned and ran.

"Devin! Stop!" yelled Nick.

It was too late. The bear watched Devin. It immediately dug its paws into the ground and sprinted after him. In a few seconds, the bear crashed into Devin, sending him to the ground.

The grizzly clawed at Devin's back and legs as Devin lay facedown in the grass.

Nick ran to help.

He knew he shouldn't get between Devin and the grizzly. Instead, he quickly found several large rocks on the ground and threw them as hard as he could at the bear.

One of the rocks hit the grizzly right in the forehead. The bear was shocked and surprised. It stopped clawing at Devin and looked up.

"Devin," yelled Nick. "I'm going to throw another rock at it. When I do, you get up and run as fast as you can!"

Nick bent down and grabbed another rock. He pulled back and flung it toward the bear. He made a direct hit. The bear turned toward Nick.

"Get up!" yelled Nick. Devin looked around. Then he pushed himself up off the ground and ran toward Andy.

"Hey bear!" yelled Nick trying to keep its attention off Devin. "Hey bear!"

Nick moved closer to the bear. He was only 20 feet away.

Then the bear dropped its head and began to bark. Suddenly it charged at Nick.

Nick quickly and calmly reached for his belt. Like a sheriff from the Old West, he grabbed his pepper spray off his hip, reached out his arm, and aimed the can at the bear. He pulled the trigger. A full, steady spray of gas shot from the can.

The spray surrounded the grizzly. It stopped and screamed, making a loud sound like an angry cat. Then the bear turned and raced toward the woods.

CHAPTER 8

★ NO NEXT TIME?

Even after the grizzly had disappeared into the trees, Nick kept staring straight ahead.

His legs suddenly gave out from underneath him. He dropped to his knees. Then he fell onto the ground.

He lay on his back, looking up at the pale blue sky. He was in shock. Everything had happened so quickly.

Nick heard rustling in the tall grass. Devin and Andy were running toward him.

"Are you okay?" Andy asked as they came closer.

"Yeah," said Nick. "I'm fine. Just in shock." He looked over at Devin. "How are you?" Nick asked.

"I'm all right," Devin said. "That thing tore up my clothes pretty good. A few scratches, I guess. But that's about it."

Devin turned around. His shirt and pants were ripped up.

"That was a close one," Nick said.

"I'm really sorry for what happened back there. I really am," Devin said.

"Don't worry about it," said Nick.

"You're not mad?" Devin asked.

"Right now I don't know what to think," said Nick, standing up. "You guys never listen to anything I say. I don't know why I waste my breath."

"Yeah, we know," said Andy. "We're really stupid sometimes."

"Yeah," said Devin. "From now on, I'm doing whatever you say."

"Next time, we'll listen to you," said Andy. "Promise."

"Too bad there won't be a next time," said Nick.

"What do you mean?" asked Devin.

"I mean, it's too bad we won't be taking any more camping trips together," said Nick.

"Why not?" asked Andy.

"You guys hate camping," said Nick. "I know that."

"That's not true," said Devin. "I like it."

"Give me a break," said Nick. "You don't have to try to make me feel good. I like camping and you guys don't. Big deal. It's fine."

"No, we like camping. Really!" said Andy. "Show him, Devin."

"Show me what?" asked Nick.

Devin walked over. He handed Nick his digital camera.

"Look at the pictures," Andy said.

Nick turned on the camera. On the camera's tiny screen was a close-up picture of some little purple wildflowers.

"What's this?" Nick asked.

Nick clicked to the next picture. It was a shot of a tiny stream flowing through dense green moss.

The next one was a picture of a mountain range. It was set against a large fluffy white cloud.

"Devin took those pictures," said Andy.

"Really?" asked Nick. He clicked through more of them.

"I took some too," said Andy. "We took most of them while you were hiking this morning."

"I'll admit it," said Devin, "I hated this whole camping trip idea. But after being out here for a couple of days, I think it's pretty awesome. I mean, look around. It's so cool! I've never seen anything like this in my life!"

"What about the football stadium?" asked Nick. "Isn't that better?"

"Well, yeah, being at the stadium is cool," said Devin. "But you can't see very many grizzly bears when you're at a football stadium."

The three guys laughed. Then Devin shook his head and looked at Nick. "Hey, man," he said. "I owe you a lot. I'm sorry for all the dumb things I've done on this trip."

"Yeah," said Andy. "What he said."

"All right," said Nick. "Enough of the mushy stuff. You guys are forgiven."

Nick smiled. Then he climbed to his feet. "What do you say we go find out if there are any trout in that lake over there?" he asked.

"If we catch some, does that mean we don't have to eat any more turkey lasagna?" asked Devin.

"You got it," said Nick, laughing.

Devin and Andy looked at each other. "Then let's fish!" Devin yelled happily.

★ ABOUT THE AUTHOR ★

Chris Kreie loves to camp with his family and has camped in dozens of places throughout the United States. Once, he saw a large grizzly bear while hiking. He was wise enough to not feed it. Chris lives in Minnesota with his wife and two children. He works as a school librarian, and in his free time he writes books like this.

★ ABOUT THE ILLUSTRATOR ★

When Sean Tiffany was growing up, he lived on a small island off the coast of Maine. Every day, from sixth grade until he graduated from high school, he had to take a boat to get to school. When Sean isn't working on his art, he works on a multimedia project called "OilCan Drive," which combines music and art. He has a pet cactus named Jim.

★ GLOSSARY ★

ban (BAN)—if there is a ban on something, you are not allowed to do it

fine (FINE)—a sum of money paid as a punishment for doing something wrong

freeze-dried (FREEZ-dryed)—if a food has been freeze-dried, the liquid has been taken out so that it will last longer. To eat it, you must first add water to the food.

habitat (HAB-uh-tat)—the place and natural conditions in which a plant or animal lives

herd (HURD)—a group of animals

illegal (ih-LEE-guhl)—against the law

permit (PUR-mit)—a written statement giving permission for something

ranger (RAYN-jur)—someone in charge of a park or forest

stake (STAYK)—a thick, pointed post that attaches a tent to the ground

thicket (THIK-it)—a thick growth of plants, bushes, or small trees

★ GET PREPARED ★

If you're going camping, you need to be prepared! Here is a list of things you'll need to bring. You might need more things too, depending on where you're going and what the weather will be like.

TENT
FOOD
CAMERA
BUG SPRAY
RAIN GEAR
SUNSCREEN
SLEEPING BAG
BOTTLED WATER
CLOTHES AND SHOES
COOKING EQUIPMENT
FISHING STUFF (if it's allowed)

★ FOR CAMPING ★

Here are some things to do before you leave:

Make sure to find out whether you'll be able to have a campfire at the campground or if there is a burning ban.

Find out what the shower and bathroom facilities are like (if there are any).

Find out what you'll need to do with your trash. Some campgrounds require you to carry it with you and throw it away after you leave. Some have trash facilities.

Make sure to read the rules and regulations of your campground. Knowing the rules before you leave will make sure that you don't accidentally break any of them.

★ DISCUSSION QUESTIONS ★

1. Why did Devin and Andy make fun of Nick? Were they right, or was Nick right?

2. Why was Nick upset when Devin and Andy started a fire when they slept on the beach?

3. If you went camping, would you want to follow the rules or do whatever you wanted? Explain your answer.

★ WRITING PROMPTS ★

1. Have you ever gone camping? If you haven't, do you want to? Write about camping. What is fun about it? What isn't fun?

2. Sometimes it can be interesting to think about a story from another character's point of view. Try writing chapter 1 from Andy's point of view. What does he see? What does he hear? How does he feel? What does he think about?

3. Nick thinks that he and his cousins are too different from each other to be friends. Have you ever made friends with someone who was different from you? What happened?

JAKE MADDOX

THE HUNTER'S CODE

STONE ARCH *Realistic Fiction*

On a hunt with his dad, Ethan discovers some dead deer left in the woods. A poacher is killing the animals for fun. Ethan knows that's against the Hunter's Code — after all, he broke that rule himself.

BY JAKE MADDOX

JAKE MADDOX

FREE CLIMB

STONE ARCH *Realistic Fiction*

When a police officer offers to bring Amir to a climbing wall outside of the city, Amir is thrilled. He meets William, who also loves climbing. But William doesn't want to learn the right way to climb, and before long, he is in serious danger.

★ INTERNET SITES ★

Do you want to know more about subjects related to this book? Or are you interested in learning about other topics? Then check out FactHound, a fun, easy way to find Internet sites.

Our investigative staff has already sniffed out great sites for you!

Here's how to use FactHound:

1. Visit *www.facthound.com*

2. Select your grade level.

3. To learn more about subjects related to this book, type in the book's ISBN number: **9781434207852**.

4. Click the **Fetch It** button.

FactHound will fetch the best Internet sites for you!